I LOVE YOU, TOO!

MICHAEL FOREMAN

ANDERSEN PRESS

Dad finished the bedtime story
and gently closed the book.
"Night, night, Little Bear. Sleep tight."
"Night, night, Dad. I love you."
"I love you, too," said Dad.

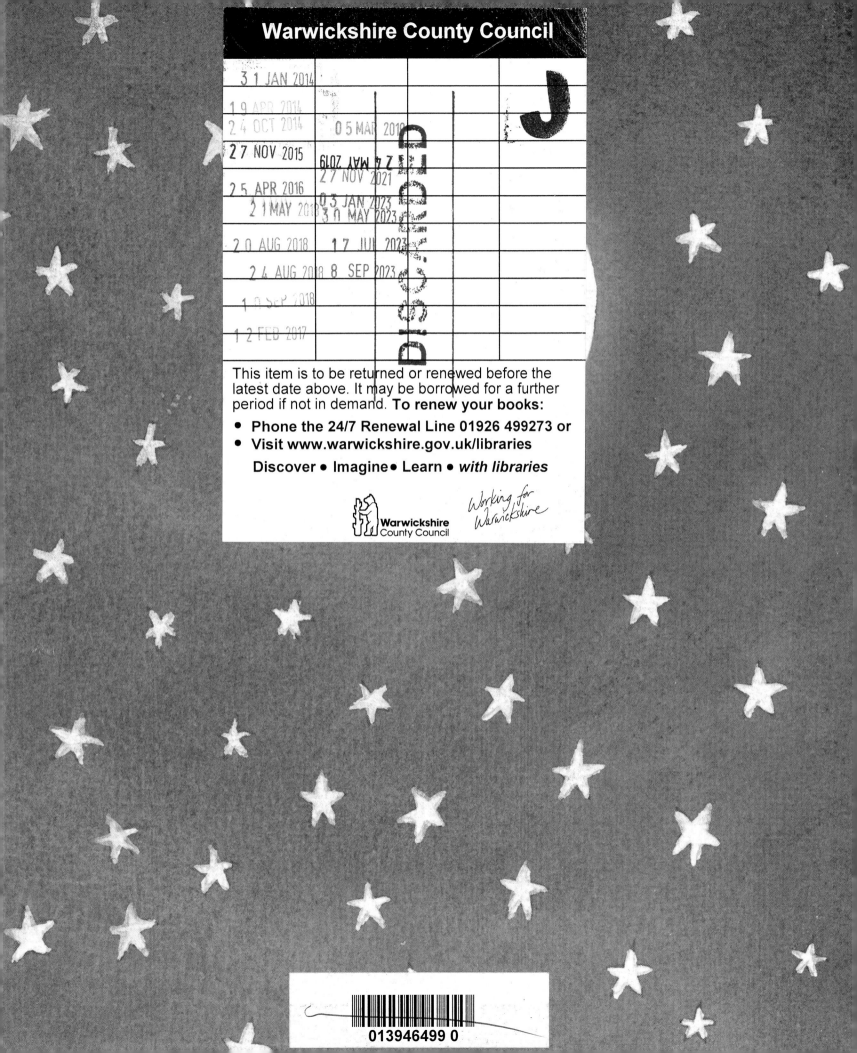

For Scout and Poppy
with love

Other books by Michael Foreman:

Fortunately, Unfortunately

Friends

Newspaper Boy and Origami Girl

Oh, If Only . . .

Superfrog!

Superfrog and the Big Stink!

Wonder Goal!

First published in Great Britain in 2013 by Andersen Press Ltd.,
20 Vauxhall Bridge Road, London SW1V 2SA.
Published in Australia by Random House Australia Pty.,
Level 3, 100 Pacific Highway, North Sydney, NSW 2060.
Copyright © Michael Foreman, 2013
The rights of Michael Foreman to be identified as the
author and illustrator of this work have been asserted
by them in accordance with the Copyright,
Designs and Patents Act, 1988.
All rights reserved.
Colour separated in Switzerland by Photolitho AG, Zürich.
Printed and bound in Malaysia by Tien Wah Press.
Michael Foreman has used watercolours in this book.

10   9   8   7   6   5   4   3   2   1

British Library Cataloguing in Publication Data available.
ISBN 978 1 84939 765 0

"I love you three," said
Little Bear, laughing.
"I love you four. Now go
to sleep," said Dad.

"I love you five," said Little Bear.
"I love you even more than that. Now
it's time to sleep," said Dad.

"I love you more than all the toys
in the toy box," said Little Bear.

"I love you more," said Dad.
"Now go to sleep."

"I love you more than all the birds
and leaves on the trees," said Little Bear.

"I love you more," said Dad.

"I love you more than all the snowflakes
of winter," said Little Bear.

"And more than all the flowers of summer."

"And more than all the grains of sand on the shore."
"I love you even more. Now go to sleep," said Dad.

"I love you more than all the fishes in the sea," said Little Bear.

"And more than all the raindrops from the sky."

"And more than all the colours of the rainbow."

"I love you even more.
Now go to sleep," said Dad.

"I love you more than all the stars in the sky," said Little Bear.

"You're only saying that because you don't want me to go downstairs," said Dad.
"No, Dad. It's because I love you."

"I love you, too," said Dad.
"I love you three . . ."
"Don't start that again, or I'll be here all night," said Dad, yawning.
"I know," said Little Bear, smiling.

Then Dad yawned again, slowly
closed his eyes and fell asleep.
Little Bear tucked him in and began
to read the book all over again . . .

"Sweet dreams, Dad."